For all my piratical nephews and great-nephews,
old and young, with a great big grubalicious
"YO HO HO!"
L. C.

First U.S. edition 2014

Library of Congress Catalog Card Number 2013955684
ISBN 978-0-7636-7399-4

14 15 16 17 18 19 GBL 10 9 8 7 6 5 4 3 2 1

Printed in Shenzhen, Guangdong, China

This book was typeset in HubbleBubble.
The illustrations were done in acrylic.

Nosy Crow
An imprint of
Candlewick Press
99 Dover Street
Somerville, Massachusetts 02144

www.nosycrow.com
www.candlewick.com

CAPTAIN BEASTLIE'S Pirate Party

Lucy Coats   Chris Mould

nosy crow
An imprint of Candlewick Press

Captain Beastlie

was the grubbiest and smelliest pirate ever to sail the seven salty seas.

But . . .

Captain Beastlie's

ship was neat and his crew
was squeaky clean.

One gray and grimsome Monday,
Captain Beastlie rolled out of bed.
"Only five days left
till m'birthday!"
he roared, picking a booger
out of his nose and flicking it.
"Take that, ye slimy
scoundrel!"

5 days

On Tuesday,
Captain Beastlie
stomped up on deck.

His socks left **pungent** patches on the **nice clean** planks. "Only **four days** left till **m'birthday!**" he bellowed, **rootling** a **glob** of peanut butter out of his ear.

4 days

"Aharr! There ye be, ye scurvy snack!"

On Wednesday, Captain Beastlie climbed the mast. His fingers left **filthy green** fungus all over the **spotless** rigging. "Only **three days** left till m'birthday!" he hollered. Just then, his holey trousers let the breeze in around his bottom.

3 days

"Scupper me sardines!
Why is it so chilly?"

howled
Captain
Beastlie.

On Thursday, Captain Beastlie yelled for the ship's cook. "Only two days left till m'birthday!" he growled. "Where's the jam for my breakfast, ye lily-livered limpet?"

"All over yer jacket, Cap'n Beastlie, sir!"
said the cook, saluting.
Captain Beastlie rubbed his
toast on his jacket, butter side down.
"Nummity-num!"

2 days

On Friday, Captain Beastlie kicked his mucky, messy clothes around the cabin. "Only one day left till m'birthday!" he cried, sniffing a filthy, rotten shirt. "Avast, m'anchovies, that's luvverly!"

1 day

Late that night, there was **rustling** and **sneaking** all over the ship as the crew tiptoed about.

Captain Beastlie snored noisily through it all.

SNORE! SNORE! SNORE!

On Saturday, Captain Beastlie woke early. "Aharr! NO days till m'birthday!" he sang loudly.

my birthday

Then he stopped and looked around his cabin.

"Blustering blood blisters! Where are all my luvverly, grubbly CLOTHES?" he yelled, leaping out of bed.

Captain Beastlie stormed out of his cabin and out onto the deck. . . .

"SCRUB-A-DUB-DUB! BIRTHDAY SURPRISE!"
shouted his crew as they grabbed him and popped
him into a **big, bubbly** tub
and gave him a
big, bubbly
scrub.

They combed out his **tangly** hair and beard . . .

and wrapped him in a **clean** towel.

Then **Captain Beastlie** spotted a brightly wrapped present.

Inside was . . .

a brand-new pirate suit
and hat.
"For he's a jolly good fellow,
For he's a jolly good fellow,

For the cap'n's a jolly good fellow . . .
And now he no longer **stinks!**"

Then they all sat down to a **great big birthday feast.**

"Cheers, m'hearties!"

growled the

cleanest, shiniest

pirate to sail the

seven salty seas . . .

until he spilled
icky-sticky crumbs
all down his
brand-new suit.